Where the Luna Moth Lands

Nicole McMann

DEDICATION

This is dedicated to the girls who dreamed.

CONTENTS

CONTENTS

ACKNOWLEDGMENTS

Through the years, my poems have been the tiny shards of life that made moments of sorrow, excitement, joy, and regret seem like tangible realities rather that otherworldly feelings I decided to ignore. The words and thoughts of this book of poetry have been a long secret love written in a notebook hidden in the backseat of my car. I want to thank everyone who supported my longwinded dreams. These dreams come to life every time someone lets my face light up with joy explaining my plans.

JUST ONE GIRL

I cannot carry the weight of the world on my shoulders
I'm just one girl,
Trying to move boulders.
I try to make sense of the world around me,
But I always end up in useless fighting.

I'm just one girl, I tell my parents, while my knees are locking
My father sometimes responds, in that "dad"
Like way he has of talking
"Gandhi was just one man, Honey. Don't sell yourself so short."
I absorb his words of wisdom,
Cling to them like they are the only tangible
Piece of hope I have left.

You expect the world of me,
But that sometimes, is just too much for me to handle.
I'm just one girl, trying not to sell myself too short.
You are my father, and honestly you are the only person
Whose opinion matters.
I just want one day to come home,
Whether it be from the USS Enterprise
Or from a one room apartment on the coast of California,
And have you thinking, she did all right, exactly what you hoped
Even though
I am just one girl. Trying

SOUTHERN MAGNOLIA

For all the summer days I sat under,
All the boy's names I carved in your skin,
And all time I spent crying, I oft wonder
If your branches still grin.
I remember those days and nights so clear
Your ears listened so gently to my tears.

Silent southern summers under
The massive magnolia made life calmer.
Feelings of sorrow felt less blue
And mountains felt less horrid, too.

I wrote summer songs on your arms,
and sang to you in the dark.
Fragrant blooms masking my secrets.
Your silent compassion consistent despite
The poems and love notes left in your bark.
Your shroud saved me from rain
And gave me haven from my deep pain.

Although I may have outgrown you,
And the words on your skin fade and hew,
There will be more to sit under your shade,
and find solace in you as you pervade.

ODE TO SOFT FLANNEL

I

Soft flannel on my wall, your colors fade.
Your threads bleached by soft light through the window.
Encased cloth held fresh life though your edges frayed.

From a place in my heart that brews sorrow,
I gaze at the wall and wonder if you
Could you have guessed that you would hold such woe?

Through pain and struggle, life enters anew!
Recalling the day, I held love most true.

II

Labor of love, they call it. I found peace
Through pain and struggle. Once I held the small
newborn body of my own wrapped in fleece.

Sweet smells filled the air; My heart felt the drawl
Of labored breathes in between deafening
Shrills. You won't remember this day at all,

But your entrance into this world filled my
Heart alone by seaside glistening skies.

III

Salt-stained boots floating on the Pacific
Haze grey and tired, the sounds of her wail
Heard through buzzing connection, horrific.

Tiny hand pressed in plaster like braille.
He traced it each night before sleep too brief.
Lines memorized; fixating on details.

Time passed like eons waiting for relief.
The first time he held her was filled with grief.

IV

Birth should be a time of joy, and wonder.
  Agony and melancholy became
The feelings that happiness hid under.

Confused by tides of emotion and shame,
  I spent time contemplating existence.
Tired, empty, swollen, bare, without aim.

How could such sorrow follow pure brilliance?
Were my thoughts mine or an unknown appearance?

V

Each winter has spring, Each night, a sunrise.
  Like tides washing salt over the forecastle,
We learn to sweep and swab salt from our eyes.

Soft flannel, no longer with your tassel,
  You held my most precious gift. she always
Was all fuss, colic. Perfectly fragile.

I learned to love that day you first breathed air.
Each day I learn more of what love can bare.

DRUNK

I'm drunk on love
That tastes so sweet.
Sweet like summer wine
Rolling on my tongue.
A tongue that would be more useful
If it could fully express
How much you intoxicate me.

I AM SORRY I HURT YOU

Looking back, I am sorry I hurt you.
I won't promise what I cannot maintain.
In youth, we're never certain what to do

Hazy lust and flowery dust. Who knew
Flowers smell the sweetest wilted in pain?
Looking back, I am sorry I hurt you.

Sweet, glazed expressions fresh with morning dew,
Memories of time we spent in spring rain.
In youth, we're never certain what to do.

Possessive and controlling, jealous too
Distortions of you lead to my disdain.
Looking back, I am sorry I hurt you.

Frigid words frozen over the last clue
Gash your mind and body over again.
In youth, we're never certain what to do.

Relearning to love will show that you grew.
The love you gave was not false or in vain.
Looking back, I am sorry I hurt you.
In youth, we're never certain what to do.

WHY I PLANT GARDENS

I love to see growth,
But I lack commitment.
I like to feel as though
My actions create and
My intentions are kind
But I confuse myself
With the words I choose.

I plant gardens,
Even though they never live
Longer than my attention allows.
At least I'll have
One tomato of effort
To show.

KISSING THE GUNNERS' DAUGHTER

As though an encore of past mistakes,
My choices seem like they
Find a way of repeating themselves.
Predictable outcomes
Often overshadowed by immediate
Gratification blinded by lust.

I'll wash the salt from
My boots, knowing I cannot
Resist the chaotic pull
The tide provides

I'll get my feet wet
Stand still,
So still
But lose control and find
Myself submerged in the
Warm embrace of the Ocean.

Predictable cycles of high and low
Do not stop my need for sand.
Waves higher than my will
Swallow my pride.
I drift further into the ocean.

Without forethought or contemplation,
I wake up after restless sleep
And kiss the Gunners Daughter again
Knowing full well, I get hurt in the
End.

LIKE A SAILOR TO THE SEA

Like a sailor to the sea
I am drawn to salt and sand
As though my soul was forged
On this impervious land

With the will of a woman
Seeking change from her past
I remember the struggles of
My grandmothers tied to the mast

Like a sailor to the sea
In times of high tide,
I find myself running full speed
Into waves, washing my soul

Decades of salt staining my sides
The mistakes made prior becoming my pyre.
Give myself patience, says the guides.
Regret and misfortune, sings the choir.

Remember me as if the struggles pass through
And bury me beneath the large Willow.

BE MY BUKOWSKI; I'LL BE O'KEEFE

Be the Bukowski of my life,
The dirty joke in my ear.
And I'll be the O'keefe on your wall
Mostly decor, lovely and small.

Be the apple pie after a late night
Moonshine and all.
I'll be the calm before the storm,
Wind and wreckage after the fall.

Be the salt on my boots,
The weathered surfaces left behind
I'll be the soft wave
Washing you clean each evening.

We'll balance each other out.
We'll annoy each other til death.
We'll love each other as two souls
Stuck in a miserable place shouldn't.

WHERE THE LUNA MOTH LANDS

Desperate for a voice
Distantly placed
Where the Luna moth lands
Becomes a place of longing
A place of silence
A place of reluctance

Vestigial remnants make yelling
An act left for those willing
To die faster

Where the Luna moth lands
Becomes a moment in time.
The time that is spent; a snapshot
Time spent by every generation before.
Stillness beginning a count down
As soon as the landing is complete
And ends as the body of the moth is used
And obsolete.

Every spring, new moths hatch.
New life begins its three part phase
Hungry and new fresh
A world of wonder.

Change begins as the silk wraps the body.
Reforming, reshaping, reconstruction
To build body anew
Metamorphosis of pieces,
Voices and choices given by others

Glistening wings emerge from silk
As this new form marks the last phase
In which motherhood
Ensures death but life becomes
Wasted without.

Where the Luna moth lands
Becomes the last stand of life.
The Luna moth never learns her fate
Until she has already peeled the silk
From herself and tried to yell.

I WISH I COULD TELL YOU IN PERSON

I wish I could tell you
What sand feels like
Bleeding between my toes
And let you see my anticipation
Of the next phrase on my lips.

I wish words meant the same
From 2,000 miles away,
And I wish that you could hear
Waves crashing on piers I sit by

I wish distance was an obscure French phrase
That meant "Mostly salty
and moist
like coastal summer rains"

Distance is time
Like tie dye shirts we left out too long,
Like those days that never ended
Waking up the next day
Wondering "Why did we let
That happen?"

Distance matures letters.
Seemingly better formulated,
And although I can't yell far enough for you
To hear me,
I'll yell until my voice is harsh
Like an 80 year old woman
Staring at the supermarket door.

I wish you find a way
To have fun, and
Rejoice in fresh mountain breezes
While I bathe in musky harbor air.
I pray you find your niche,
I hope the best for you, and all
Your dreams come true, because
This world is hard enough
Without being stomped down to nothing,
And you have more heart than I have ever seen.
A gift from someone long past.
Passion bleeding from every pore.
Hard work in what you love.
And I wish you to never lose that.

SWOLLEN HEART

I want to be a pulse,
A living, breathing want
I want to oscillate in tones
Unheard by humans before us.

I want to be a sigh on a cold morning.
The half empty beer on your night stand,
Your one night stand
That doesn't end.
A fresh journey,
Always new, and never in the same place.
I want to kiss your skin
Like a summer sun
Leaving freckles as proof of my
Love.

You sweat tastes salty and harsh,
And I know that one day
Your boots will be covered in hate
Fresh from the sea,
But my freckles are fresher,
And my sighs still sound the same.

They sink to the floor,
Flooding the room with every breath.
Sighs that keep our secrets safe.
Sighs that I cannot fully explain,
But mean I trust you

YOU ARE PRETTY

We all want to be pretty.
We all want to be a glistening beacon of desire.
We all want to turn heads when
We grace a room with our presence
As though Aphrodite herself had entered.

No matter how many men treat you poorly,
or how many people look at you nasty,
You stride down nasty cobblestone walkways
With the pride of a true Goddess.
You are pretty.

A pretty that doesn’t have
To be perfect.
Your pretty is uniquely flavored.
A pretty that burns the tongue,
But soothes the soul.

The pretty the world expects from you
Is fed to you from a spoon
You will never get to enjoy.
Pretty isn't fueled by a hungry monster
That tricks you into thinking
Love means lust.

So remember, you're a pretty that sings in the morning.
A type of pretty that truly listens.
The type of pretty that smells like rosemary
And lavender on Sunday mornings.

Dear, you are pretty
Just don't forget that.

I’ve been fucked up
About your death for a while.
Not the kind that keeps you up crying
But stabs your dreams.

I’ll think about pieces of myself
Left in the back seat
Of that Honda odyssey
And remember the pain
You routinely caused me.

I wake up in sweats
Dreaming about the lives
we could be living
Had you been kind and gentle
As though these delusions are capable of
Replacing misery like tokens on a mantle.

But you decided
The day I entered this world
Simultaneously, the best day
For you to leave it.
So every year, I celebrate
Having a lifetime free
From your voice booming,
Your fists slamming,
And me crying in that backseat.

TIME

I watch you age.
I watch you age in my dreams
Where the laws of space
And time don't apply.
I watch you age even though
Your body is becoming one with the Earth.

Your laugh is the same,
Oddly.
It's though these vivid pictures
Found a place in space
That you're still alive
And trick me into watching
From eyes not my own.

ON THE DAY I HAD MY FIRST CHILD

A lot of mothers will
Tell you,
The first feeling
They felt
Was
love.

I felt
Fear.

A WOMAN OF IRON AND SILK

As you grow, I hope
You can remember me
As a woman of iron
And silk.
A woman filled
With fierce love.
A woman that smells
Like soup simmering, lilac blooms, wet Earth.
A woman that gives
Everything she has for you.
A woman that will love
You no matter what.
But most importantly,
A woman who wasn't
Perfect,
But tried so hard regardless

FLAG POLES

Touch,
Touch,
Touch,
Skip.
Touch.

Pause.
Breathe,
Restart.

Touch,
Touch,
Touch…..

OPHELIA

Does it hurt to drown?
I find myself in a deep dive,
An eternal search for relief.
The time spent finding the answer
Makes the steam turn cool.

Is it worse?
Worse than worry.
Worse than being the constant
And never-ending annoyance
Like a hang nail,
Will it hurt to tear the nail away?
How much must pull
Before cords unravel into
Dozens of wisps
Sheer and strained.

The cool water pulls
Pulls me in.
The pull feels like a forbidden love.
A summer filled with fleeting heat.
Eternal summer pulling my head underwater
Floating in space and time for a moment
As relief materializes.
As silence settles.
As the last of the worry
Floats to the surface
Ophelia calls for me as we float together
Downstream.

ABOUT THE AUTHOR

Growing up moving around meant making the best of change. I found so much relief in literature, but mostly poetry. From the Midwest to the South, my life's adventure landed me in Southeast Nebraska with a lovely husband, two monsters of children, and more chickens that I ever thought I would have. The real gift of my life has been the love and support of my friends and family. I am thankful everyday to have people who love me in this world. Recent projects in the arts for me have been butterfly wing paintings and The Naptime Debrief Podcast with Meg Engel. On there we discuss life, motherhood, and feeling human when you feel drained to your core. I have also developed a love for terrible kindle unlimited werewolf novels and refuse to quit them. My life has been a gift every moment, even the hard ones.

www.ingramcontent.com/pod-product-compliance
Lightning Source LLC
LaVergne TN
LVHW040937150826
845672LV00008B/2399

* 9 7 9 8 3 6 6 5 4 4 1 7 7 *